First published in the United States of America in January 2015 by Bloomsbury Children's Books
www.bloomsbury.com

Bloomsbury is a registered trademark of Bloomsbury Publishing Plc

For information about permission to reproduce selections from this book, write to Permissions, Bloomsbury Children's Books, 1385 Broadway, New York, New York 10018
Bloomsbury books may be purchased for business or promotional use. For information on bulk purchases please contact Macmillan Corporate and Premium Sales Department at
specialmarkets@macmillan.com

Library of Congress Cataloging-in-Publication Data
Good, Jason.
Must. Push. Buttons!/by Jason Good ; illustrated by Jarrett Krosoczka.
pages   cm
Summary: Illustrations and simple text reveal what a toddler is thinking while going through a typical day.
ISBN 978-1-61963-095-6 (hardcover) • ISBN 978-1-61963-239-4 (e-book) • ISBN 978-1-61963-240-0 (e-PDF)
[1. Toddlers—Fiction. 2. Thought and thinking—Fiction. 3. Humorous stories.] I. Krosoczka, Jarrett, Illustrator. II. Title.
PZ7.G59967Mus 2015   [E]—dc23   2014013155

Art created digitally by assembling acrylic paints, watercolors, and oil pastels • Typeset in GMMedallion • Book design by Yelena Safronova

Printed in China by Leo Paper Products, Heshan, Guangdong
1 3 5 7 9 10 8 6 4 2

All papers used by Bloomsbury Publishing, Inc., are natural, recyclable products made from wood grown in well-managed forests.
The manufacturing processes conform to the environmental regulations of the country of origin.

To Lindsay, Silas, and Arlo —J. G.

For Dominick and Anthony —J. J. K.

You really want to know what he's thinking? . . .

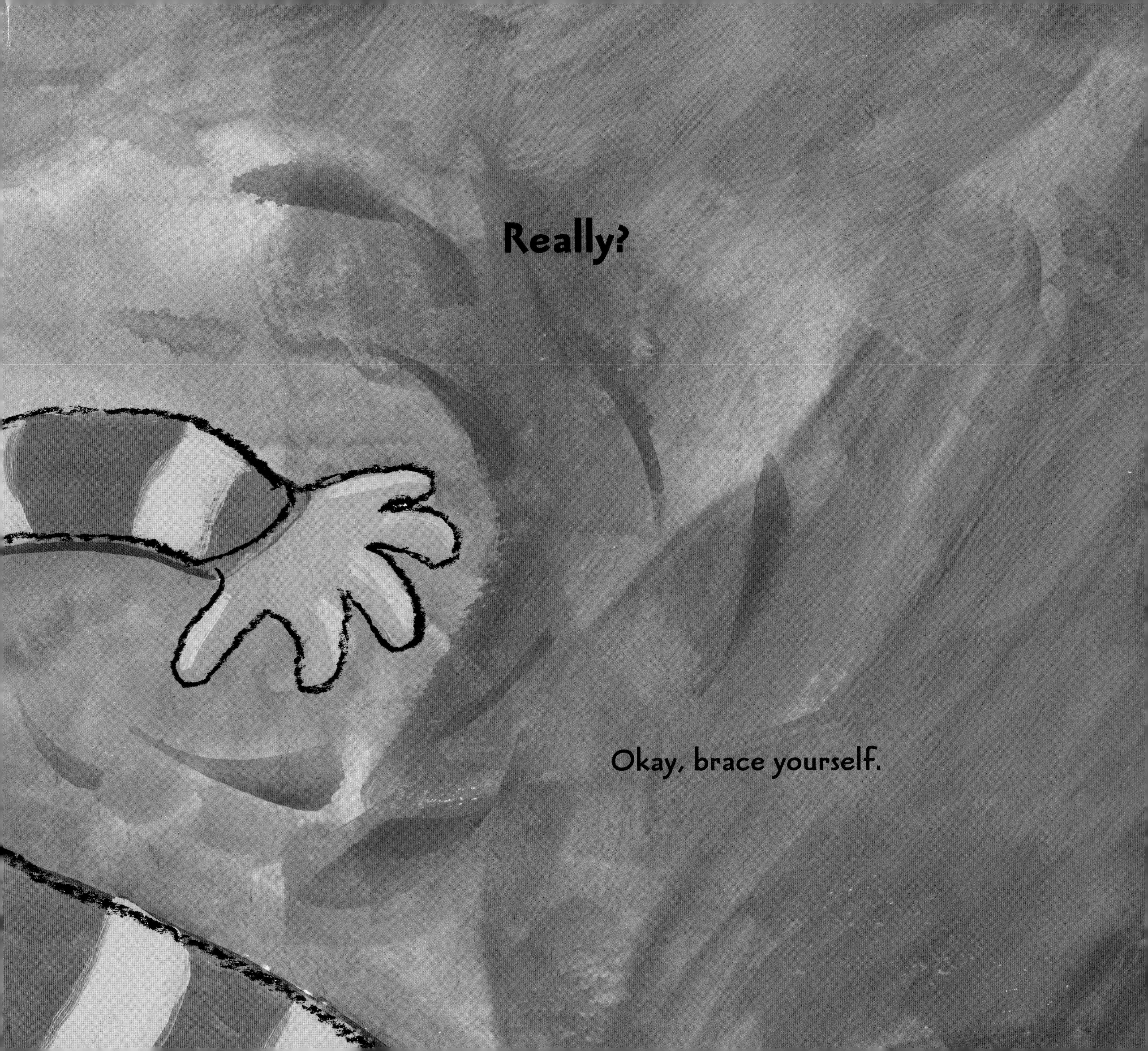

Really?

Okay, brace yourself.

I wanna play with Daddy's phone.

I wanna put on Mommy's shoes.

TAP, TAP, TAP

Get Mommy's shoes off my feet now!

I wanna turn the microwave on and off.

I wanna open and close the refrigerator.

I need to push some buttons . . .

I wanna pick up the cat by its head.

I wanna throw all the toothbrushes in the sink.

Wait, I'm REALLY hungry.

No, you did **not** just give me fruit.

CHEDDAR BUNNIES.

I'm thirsty.

No, not for that.

Yes, perfect, juice box.

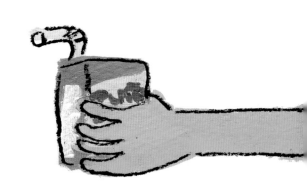

I'M GONNA SQUEEZE

THIS THING ALL OVER MYSELF.

Now my pants are wet.

Wow, is that my toe?

Wait, where's Daddy?

Where's the cat?

Where's Mommy?

MOMMY LEFT **FOREVER!**

Oh, there she is. I wanna play with her phone.

I wanna go for a walk, but I don't wanna go outside.

No, not inside either!

I'm tired.

I'm not tired.

This shirt itches.

STOP ASKING ME IF I'M TIRED.

I wanna put on that awesome song that annoys you.

What is UP with my shirt?

Where's the toy that goes BEEP, BEEP, BEEP?

I NEED TO PUSH

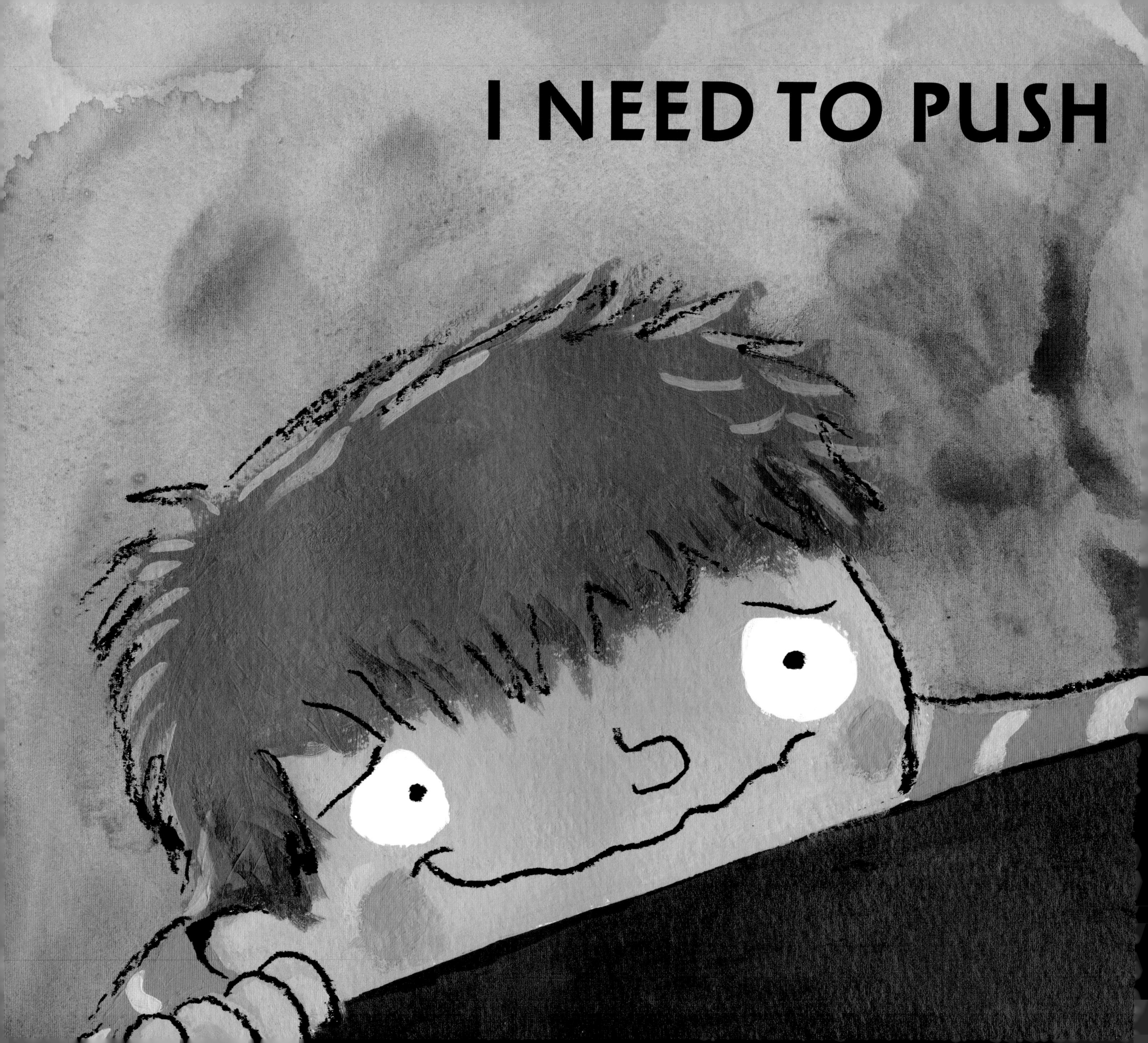

SOME BUTTONS . . .

Oh look, a new person. I wonder if he has a phone.

You did NOT just try to take off my shirt again!

Did I hear a dog bark?

Where's the dog?

Wait, do we have a dog?

I WANNA SEE A DOG NOW!

Never mind. I wanna play with the iPad.

I think I peed.

I'm bored.

If I could just play with
Daddy's pho . . .